i

ii

Cousin

Don Allen

ISBN: 979-8-9906053-0-5

eISBN: 979-8-9906053-1-2

Publisher: Don Allen

Also, by Don Allen

1 A Quiet Morning

I was spending a quiet morning with my son, ltl' George and Maggi, my significant other. Looking at him, I was amazed he was almost four years old. "Where has the time gone," I thought.

I had just returned from my most recent GIS assignment, which left me stranded on a sinking barge in the Indian Ocean, morphing into a reunion with Fat Leonard in Singapore and eventually into an MI-6 tasking in Zimbabwe—or, as Magie would tell you, eighteen months of galivanting.

The time was not all a loss. An investment in a Zimbabwe gold mine resulted in a substantial inflow of cash into the Basdakis Shipping Brockage bank account. Maggi, as the firm's CEO, did not object.

BSB was my company or was until I asked Maggi to manage it. She had two conditions: BSB would be legit, I would cut ties with my Uncle Christos's antique smuggling operations, and she would get 40 percent ownership. The company has thrived under her management, and she is now a respected member of the Greek Shipping Association.

"You need to stay home," she said. "Next time your Uncle Alexander calls, tell him you are busy."

My uncle, Uncle Alexander, was the number two person in the Greek Intelligence Service, heavily relied on by the Director, Constance Gabris. He is the oldest of the four Basdakis brothers. My father and two younger brothers were members of the resistance movement against Georgios Papadopoulos's dictatorship in the early 70s. Alexander, on the other hand, joined the state security forces. 'blood' overruled duty, and he facilitated his siblings' escape to Italy. Under subsequent administrations, he became the keeper of personnel dossiers that senior government officials preferred to be kept secret.

Several years earlier he roped me into a mission to Cyprus which ended up putting me in the hospital and killing my best friend. Nicholas, Uncle Christos's son, and I grew up together in Biloxi, Mississippi. As teenagers, we both dabbled in questionable activities. A judge convinced Nicholas the Army was calling him. I went on to college with an ROTC scholarship and served my country for four years as a naval officer before being asked to leave after an unfortunate firefight in the Persian Gulf where I sunk four Iranian speedboats.

My adventure on Cyprus was followed by the GIS 'loaning' me to MI-5. On a positive note, that mission introduced me to Lord Ashford, my great-uncle. My task was to protect Ashford after his repeated rejection of an MI-5 security detail. The threat was from a group of Scottish nationalists who took issue with Ashford's position on a united, United Kingdom. I failed. We came upon the sniper moments after he fired. In the ensuing gunfire, my MI-5 partner was killed. Lord Ashford was the retired Commander of the 3rd Gurkha Rifles, loved by 'his' men. The resulting slaughter of the Scottish nationalists – well that's another story.

Magdalen, Maggi, is my significant other. We flirted with the idea of marriage a few times, but she does not want to give up the freedoms she has as a single lady in Greek society. She has taken on my reform as her personal cause. When we first met, a set up by Nicholas's wife Elena, Nicholas and I had a thriving business dealing in pilfered antiquities. It was this business that attracted Uncle Alexander; he needed a man in Cyprus to retrieve information on Turkish military deployments from his spy. An archaeological dig was the perfect cover. I had a previous history with Dr. Brown from Manchester University, buying newly unearthed artifacts. He was conveniently conducting an archaeological dig in the Turkish-controlled area of Cyprus– well, that's another story also.

My cell chirped. Maggi said, "Don't answer it; it will be your uncle." I let the call go to voice mail. After some time, she said, "You might as well listen to it; you'll be distracted the rest of the morning if you don't."

I brought up the stored messages and selected the most recent. To my surprise, it was Alexander. I was expecting a call from Corfu's mayor regarding BSB's request for more dock space in the city's port.

"George, call me when you can. Your cousin Isabell's body was found yesterday on a London backstreet."

Maggi and I looked at each other with the same question, "Cousin?"

2 Cousin Isabell

As far as I knew I had no cousins in England. Lord Ashford had no children.

"It's a ploy to get you involved in another of his misadventures," said Maggi.

"You're probably right," I said as I mentally reviewed Lord Ashford's family history.

My maternal grandmother was related to the Greek royal family. Her Uncle was the Count of Thessaloniki. His son Mathew, my mother's cousin, had two children, Jennifer and Winston. Jennifer, the older of the two, married Lord Humboldt of Lincolnshire. They had no children. That leaves Winston, my 1st cousin, once removed. Upon his retirement, as the Regimental Commander of the 3rd Gurkha Rifles, he was Knighted, becoming Lord Ashford. He never married.

Curiosity got the better of me. I told Maggi I had to call Alexander. As she rolled her eyes, I got Alexander on the line. "What do you mean, my cousin Isabell?"

"If you come to Athens, I'll explain."

"I can't; it's ltl George's birthday party this weekend. He'll be four. Why don't you come and join us? It's not every day your great-great-nephew turns four."

Maggi added, "Uncle Alexander, we would love to see you. It's been ages since you visited."

After a short pause, "How can I turn down an invitation from a beautiful woman? I accept."

George's party was on Saturday afternoon. Invited were his playschool friends and other close friends of the family.

Elena, Nicolas's widow and a close friend of Maggi's, would be at the party. It was with Alexander's encouragement that Nicolas accompanied me to Cyprus where he was killed. "How is Elena going to react to Alexander's presence?" I asked Maggi.

"She'll be fine. She knows it was Nicolas's decision to go. If she blames anyone, it is Brown with his promise of gold."

***

Elena arrived early on Saturday, intending to help Maggi prepare for the party, which was totally unneeded. Ltl' George was a fixture at the BSB office. Whenever Maggi went to work, he was with her. The office staff had taken over the party setup.

I invited Elena to join me on the patio. It was my job for the morning to stay out of the way and entertain Elena. I offered her coffee and 'fat-free' Greek pastries.

"I'll take the coffee and only dream of fat-free pastries," she said. "But while we are sitting here, I'll give you the small gift I brought you."

Elena pulled out what looked to be a scroll from her large handbag and handed it to me. "I've started a new business," she said. "Elena's Genealogy Research. You know, more and more people want to find their ancestors, and I've gotten quite good at ferreting out birth and death records and an occasional family secret. It pays well. I earn almost as much as my father does with Vrettos Antiques."

"This is your family tree. You're at the bottom, followed by your parents and their parents. Here is Nicholas, your four brothers, and at the top, on your mother's side, Count Thessaloniki. And coming down that line, we find Lord Ashford."

I'm familiar with my mother's side of the family, but my father's side is a mystery.

"Nikolaos Basdakis is your grandfather. He was an officer in the Greek army after World War I.

"There was a promise made by the British Prime Minister that Greece would gain territory from the Ottoman Empire after the war. The Turks did not agree. We invaded Anatolia in 1919. In 1922, we were soundly defeated. Prince Andrew was held responsible for the defeat, and that is why he fled the country and your mother's uncle followed him. Your grandfather, Nikolaos Basdakis, was also a scapegoat, accused of dereliction of duty, resulting in one of the fronts collapsing and the loss of five hundred Greek lives. He was eventually exonerated by the military, but the humiliation scared him for the rest of his life. He married your grandmother, Ophelia, in 1932, and they had four sons."

Looking at it, all I can say is, "This is amazing. I'm going to get it framed. Thank you."

Uncle Alexander arrived later that morning and was ushered out to the patio to join Elena and me. They greeted each other, and although Elena maintained a friendly disposition, I could tell she'd prefer other company. While in the kitchen refilling the coffee carafe, I asked Maggi if she would rescue Elena, perhaps tasking her to work with the group decorating the party area.

Now that Alexander and I were alone, "Tell me about this cousin," I said.

"As you know, your mother's Uncle was the Count of Thessaloniki. He fled Greece, along with other Royals when the monarchy was abolished early in the last century. His son Mathew was one of Prince Phillips's playmates in the '30s. Mathew maintained ties with the royal family and is rumored to have saved Prince Philip's life during the war. After Mathew's death toward the end of the war, the Prince took it upon himself to look after Mathew's two children, Jennifer and Winston. Winston, as you know, became Lord Ashford.

"As far as we knew, Mathew was the Count's only child. Jennifer, Mathew's daughter, had no children, and his son Winston never married. Now that leaves us with a mystery: who is this Isabell that the British authorities claim is your cousin?"

Holding up the family tree that Elena had just given me, "There is no Isabell in this tree," I said.

Alexander continued, "It appears that a dalliance with a minor royal family member, the viscountess of Hinsdale, at the start of Winston's military career resulted in Rupert, born in the early '50s. For whatever reason, Winston did not marry the countess, and in fact, their relationship became quite frosty over the years. Rupert was an embarrassment to all and not mentioned."

"Rupert became a member of the Mediterranean jet set in the '90s. Rupert's mother died in 2007, making Rupert a vice-count. At some point, Rupert met and married a stunning Lebanese beauty. Together, they produced Isabell. Isabell inherited her mother's beauty and her father's carefree ways."

"Lord Ashford never acknowledged Rupert, his wife, or their daughter."

Looking at Alexander, all I could say was, "Lord Ashford never mentioned any of this during my time with him."

7

Alexander resumed my family history. "Isabell was a member of London's Generation Z, the Zoomers. She was found dead on a London back street last month. She was reported to be a party girl. It is not known if she was murdered to prevent embarrassment to a prominent government official. Or did her death have something to do with her Lebanese uncle, a weapons dealer?"

"Okay, this is all very interesting, but what does it have to do with me?"

"Well, due to her uncle's potential involvement and her royal lineage, MI-6 was asked to work with the police. Sir George, one of MI-6's mandarins, recommended that the Greek Intelligence Service be brought into the loop since we are currently tracking Mideast weapon dealers for NATO."

"No! I'm just settling down to a quiet family life. Maggi will kill me."

"Since you knew Lord Ashford and have worked with MI-5 and Scotland Yard, Sir George has requested your assistance."

"What assistance?" Maggi said as she joined us on the patio, giving Alexander a wary look.

3 London

I was met at Heathrow by Sir George's driver and taken to my hotel, The Carlton Tower. "Sir George has taken care of all the expenses, sir," said the driver. "If it's convenient, he would like to meet with you at eight tomorrow morning in his office."

"Yes, thank you," I said as the doorman took my carry-on bag. Convenient, I'm thinking. If I'm late, his people will collect me.

The Carlton Tower Hotel was just off Hyde Park and room rates had to be upward of four hundred pounds a night.

MI-6 was located in the Secret Intelligence Service Building on the south side of the Thames, squeezed between the Vauxhall rail yard and the river. The taxi had me there by 7:45.

I found Sir George's suite of offices. As one of the secretaries offered to get me coffee, Sir George appeared and invited me into his private office, which had a spectacular view of the river and the city skyline.

The young lady followed us into the office with a coffee service. "George, as I recall, you are addicted to coffee. Help yourself; there should be cream and sugar there."

With coffee in hand, I sat in the overstuffed chair Sir Geroge pointed to in the seating group by the window. He started to take the chair across from me when his secretary escorted Commander Milo in.

"Commander, good of you to join us. There is coffee there if you like, or I can get you tea if you prefer."

"Coffee is fine," he said as he prepared his cup, more like milk with coffee flavoring.

"Good morning, George," he said addressing me. "What's it been, two years?"

"Thereabouts," I responded. It was a bit more than two years ago when Sarah Wilson was shot and died in my arms. Sarah was one of Milo's agents. We were Lord Ashford's protection detail. We failed, and Sarah was dead.

"Well let's not dwell on the unfortunate past," said Sir George, "We have Isabell to talk about."

"George, I asked Alexander to loan you to us again to help solve Isabell's murder. You knew Lord Ashfield in his last days and may have some insights to offer Scotland Yard's investigation. You are also with the Greek Intelligence Service, which has an ongoing investigation into Mideast arms dealers.

"I believe Alexander has briefed you on Isabell's background. Was she killed by a government official she was having an affair with or by her Lebanese uncle, who we believe to be an arms dealer? I'd like you to work with Commander Milo. If she was killed by the former, Scotland Yard will take care of it. If by her uncle, your role will become more active."

As Milo and I left the MI-6 facilities, Milo invited me to meet with the Scotland Yard Inspector working the case.

His car met us at the front of the building. I thought he intended us to go to his office. MI-5 was housed in a new building on the other side of the river, not far from Westminster, nearly across the river from MI-6. I observed that the sister agencies could run a ferry service between the two, beating road traffic. It was normally a short trip, but Milo explained we were going to the new Metropolitan Police building, affectionately called the MET and by others as the New Scotland Yard, located another half mile down the river.

As we passed through a bank of metal detectors, a middle-aged police inspector met us. "Detective Chief Inspector Allenby," he said, introducing himself. "You must be George Basdakis. That was quite a knife fight you set off in Glasglow. We're still talking about it."

The knife fight he was referring to was Lord Ashford's Gurkhas exacting vengeance on Ashford's assassins.

"It wasn't so much as a fight as it was a massacre," I said, "at least that's what the papers reported."

4 Scotland Yard

DCI Allenby escorted us to his office on the third floor. His view of the Thames was less spectacular than that of Sir George's and featured the south side of London, which in years past hosted the tawdrier aspects of city life.

As he got us seated and his secretary dispatched to find coffee, I asked the DCI, "Any relation to Field Marshel Allenby?"

"Yes, he is my great-uncle," said Allenby. "Why?"

"No reason. I'm a history buff and your name just made me curious. Sorry for the distraction."

"Here's the coffee service," he said. "Help yourself, then let's get down to business."

As we were taking our places around the conference table, a youngish man joined us. "This is Detective Inspector Harold Lynn; he's doing much of the leg work and knows as much about Isabell as anyone," said Allenby.

"Harold, this is George Basdakis, on loan to us from MI-6. He's here to observe," he said looking at me. "If we find Isabell's uncle is involved with her death, George will be taking the lead."

"What we know at this point," said Allenby, "is that Isabell was murdered late Saturday night or early Sunday morning two weeks ago. Her body was found when the dumpster bins were being emptied. She was found behind one. The autopsy showed she had been strangled by a thin rope or garrote. It took us several days to identify the body. She had no identification on her. Once identified, we contacted her father, Baron Hinsdale. Given his connection to the royal Household, the case was assigned to me."

"Now, to make this case more interesting, it appears our Miss. Hinsdale was twenty-three years old, and she was a party girl. She was frequently seen on the arm of one or another member of Parliament. Harold has been interviewing these MPs," Allenby said as he looked at Harold.

Not missing a beat, Harold continued, "Almost to a man they claimed Isabell was just a casual acquaintance, confirmed by their staff, or a family friend, and also confirmed by Baron Hinsdale, with the exception of two. One claimed he didn't know her despite the photo in the Times gossip section showing them together. And the second, we are still trying to locate."

"These last two MPs," I asked, "what committees are they on? Have they taken positions on any controversial issues? Can they be compromised?"

"We are still looking into that," said Harold.

"And boyfriends?" Milo asked.

"Not that we know of," said Allenby. Harold interviewed her neighbors; Isabell had a flat in Mayfair, and none remembered seeing any male visitors."

"And females?" I asked.

"Just two, both from Woodstock and Sons, a public relations company where Isabell worked. We are in the process of interviewing them."

As the meeting was winding to an end, I asked if it would be a problem if I talked to Isabell's family and other people of interest.

DCI Allenby gave Milo a look, who nodded and answered, "It should be okay. DI Lynn will take you around."

As we were leaving, DI Lyne came up and said, "I was very sorry to hear about Sarah Wilson. We went through the police academy together. She was a good person."

"I was with her when she died you know. A few seconds earlier both she and Lord Ashford would be alive today."

"If you have time, there is a deli nearby where we can get a kosher ham sandwich and talk."

"Kosher ham?"

"Okay, it's a liberal Jewish deli that caters to its goy customers," he said, "but the sandwich is to die for."

"Milo, are you going to join us? Harold asked.

"No, I have to get back to the office, defend the realm against foreign threats you know."

5 Baron Hinsdale

"Harold, What can you tell me about Rupert Hinsdale?"

"First, Hinsdale is his hereditary fiefdom. Rupert's last name is Windsor, taken from his mother. He is a distant relative of the Queen. Other than that, he is in his late 50s, in good health, and a rather likable chap. His wife, Nadine, also in her 50s, retains her youthful looks, but I suspect with some help. She is standoffish but friendly once she gets to know you. They were both devastated by Isabell's death."

"I'd like to meet them. Can you set that up?" I asked. "And what can you tell me about the two MPs you mentioned earlier?"

"Well, the first, John Bricklayer, represents a district near Bermingham. I have pretty much ruled him out. He claims he has no knowledge of the picture in the Times or even attending that event. Talking with his staff and family, it appears John is a serious alcoholic. After a few drinks, he has no idea where he is or why he's there, but to others, he appears normal—the definition of a politician."

"The second MP is more interesting. He represents the paki community in Leeds. Sorry, the proper term is Pakistani. Anyway, Afram Gurmani was elected to Parliament five years ago. One of the committees he's on works with the UN's nonproliferation of weapons team in the Mideast. Afram Gurmani has not been seen since Isabell's body was found.

"I understand Isabell was a party girl. And you know of no boyfriends. What about her nightlife activities? I asked.

"Her friends at work said she liked the hangouts around Soho and Covent Gardens, many friendly to the LGBT community. We don't know which way Isabell swung. I have two sergeants questioning proprietors and frequent customers to get leads. So far no one admits to knowing Isabell."

"This girl appears to have led a double life, a work life and a nightlife, with little overlap between the two," said Harold.

DI Lyne looked at his watch, "I have to get back to the precinct— an all-hands meeting. Perhaps there will be more on Isabell. I'll call her parents and try to set up a meeting for you tomorrow." And with that, he was off.

***

The next morning Harold collected me at my hotel, and we headed up the M11 motorway. "Where to?" I asked.

Cambridge, Isabell's parents live in Grantchester, a small village on the town's outskirts.

Ninety minutes later we were pulling up to a modest Tudor home. Modest might be an understatement considering the landscaping and imposing facade.

As Harold was about to ring the bell, the door opened, and my jaw fell. Standing in front of me was a young version of Lord Ashford.

He invited us in, saying, "Nadine will be down shortly."

We were ushered into a small sitting room as Harold introduced me. "This is George Basdakis. MI-5 asked him to assist in solving

16

Isabell's murder. Mr. Basdakis has some foreign contacts that might prove useful … and he knew your father."

The Baron turned to me, "First, please call me Rupert. I'm not one for formalities. And yes, I know of you. Although my father never contacted me, I did follow him. He led a rather active life after he left my mother. He was gone before I was born, you know. My mother was always bitter, not at him, but at the system that forced them apart. She held the Queen responsible."

"Sorry for airing family laundry," he said, "but I thought I needed to get that out of the way."

"Yes, thank you," I said as an elegant lady entered the room. Standing, "Nadine I presume; I am so sorry for your loss. I'm George Basdakis, and I have been asked by MI-5 to work with the MET to find Isabell's killer."

As she sat, "Did Rupert offer you any refreshment?" At this point, Rupert got up and called the maid, requesting that she bring in the coffee and tea service, which was apparently waiting in the hallway.

Looking at Rupert, I said, "You know we are related, don't you? Second or third cousins. Your great-grandfather, the Count of Thessaloniki, was my mother's uncle."

"No, my mother either never knew or chose not to tell me anything of my father's family. After we've solved Isabell's murder, I'd like to know more."

Okay, let's start. What can you tell me about Isabell? Did she have any close friends? School friends? What do you know of her life in London?"

"There was one girl Isabell was close to, Karen Wilson," said Nadine. "We sent Isabell to a boarding school, *The Nunnery* in York. As a young teen, Isabell was more than we could manage. Karen,

17

about the same age, was sent there for the same reason. I believe the Wilsons live in Edinburgh. The two formed a tight teenage bond."

"Do you have their address?" I asked.

"No. But I'm sure you can get it from the school."

I looked at Harold and saw that he was putting this information in his notebook.

What about London? Why did she move there, and what do you know of her activities?"

"Very little," said Rupert. After leaving *The Nunnery* she wanted nothing to do with us."

My uncle Amal remained in touch with her. They always had a close relationship," said Nadine.

"Where can we find Amal?" asked Harold.

"Right now, I don't know. He is always traveling: Beirut, Ciro, Damascus, and other cities. He's in London two or three times a year. He's in the import-export business and is always on the move looking for a deal."

"Please let us know the next time he is in England," said Harold.

Looking at the two, I asked, "Is there anything in your past that might have precipitated Isabell's murder?"

Rupert, looking somewhat embarrassed, said, "You probably know of my 'carefree' life as a young man. I think out of guilt, my mother didn't reign me in, and I squandered the small inheritance my grandmother left me. Flitting around the Mediterranean, I always had to have the biggest boat in the harbor. I met Nadine in Cannas; she was a calming influence."

"He was besotted with me," said Nadine. "I told him I'd have nothing to do with him until he sold his 'big' boat. He sold the boat,

18

returned to school, is now a professor, and heads the Department of English Studies at Cambridge."

"And you Nadine?" asked DI Lynn.

"Not much to tell. My father was very successful in starting his business in the Christian section of Beirut. After the revolt in the '60s, he built up his business. In the '70s he married, and I came along. During the unpleasantness of the late 80s, he sent my mother and me to live in Marseilles where he and my uncle, his brother Amal, had some business connections. This always seemed strange to me given Amal was a practicing Muslim and my father was a 'weekend' Christian. My father was killed in the '90s when Israel invaded Lebanon—killed by Hezbollah gunfire. Rupert and I met, as he said, in Cannes in the mid-90s. He changed his ways; we got married, and Isabell was born on June 10th, 1998."

6 The Bastard

As we neared the end of our interview, Rupert asked that I tell him what I knew of his father's family.

I can only give you the high points I learned when I was with him," I said.

"Prince Philip, Duke of Edinburgh, consort to Queen Elizabeth, was born on Corfu in 1921. His family was exiled from the country when Philip was eighteen months old after Greece's humiliating defeat by the Turks in the Greco-Turkish War.

"Our grandmother was related to the Count of Thessaloniki. When Philip's family was forced into exile, the Count and his family joined the royal exodus. His youngest son Mathew, my mother's cousin, your grandfather, was one of Philip's closest childhood friends. In 1939, Mathew joined the Royal Navy and served alongside the Prince in the early years of the war. It's believed Mathew saved Philip's life when their ship was torpedoed in the North Atlantic. Mathew was later killed near the end of the war. Prince Philp took on the role of guardian for Mathew's children, Jennifer and Winston. Your grandmother died in the early 40s. I don't know her name. Jennifer married Lord Humboldt of Lincolnshire in the late 40s. That brings us to your father.

"Winston had a distinguished career with the British Army. With Philip's recommendation, he was commissioned as a second lieutenant in the Cheshire Regiment in 1951. The following year the Regiment was dispatched to Malaysia to help quell the Malayan Emergency, a communist insurgency.

"The regimental headquarters was located in Penang Province. Attached to the First Brigade were the 2nd Gurkha Rifles.

"Winston was so impressed with the Gurkhas he requested to be transferred to one of their regiments. Postings were hard to get.

"Upon his return to England, Winston approached the Prince requesting his help. It wasn't Philip's endorsement that got Winston the transfer; it was the recommendation he received from Sargent Narayan Shah of the 2nd Gurkha Rifles, whom Winston had befriended.

"Winston spent the next thirty years with the Gurkhas, rising to Regimental Commander with the rank of Colonel. Wounded twice, he earned their respect by leading from the front. Upon retirement, he was Knighted, becoming Lord Ashford. He bought a small manor house in Windermere, in the Lake District, not far from Manchester.

"He was assassinated two years ago. You may have read about it. His men exacted justice on the assassins, a Scottish extremist group.

"The family name was originally Servopoulos. Your father's family name is de Courcy, a Norman name. Your grandfather found the name Servopoulos a detriment to his advancement in English society. He changed his name to de Courcy. Mathew was not one to go halfway. He chose a name that went back to 1066; he out-snobed the snobs."

"Now tell me what you know," I said.

"My father had an affair with my mother in 1950. She was the Vice-Countess of Hinsdale. When it became known she was pregnant, she was shipped off to Holyrood Castel in Scotland, and my father disappeared. From your history of my father, it sounds like Prince Philip hustled him into the army and had him posted halfway around the world.

"My mother was forbidden to ever contact him again. Rumors that I later heard mentioned threats against my father if he contacted her; he'd face the end of his career and jail time for deflowering a member of the royal family. I don't think the two ever saw each other again.

"I grew up in the arms of luxury. I attended Cambridge University but dropped out in the '80s to join the jet set in the Mediterranean. My mother, I guess, out of guilt, funded my escapades. In the early 90s, I met Nadine. She brought me back to reality. Mother was quite pleased with her, given that Nadine had tamed me. I went back to University and completed my studies, earning a doctorate in English history. I am now a professor at Cambridge.

"My mother was always bitter about the way the Queen treated her. She even declined an invitation to serve as a lady in waiting in the '60s, which would have opened many doors for her.

"She died eight years ago, bitter to the end. Upon her death, I should have become the Vice-Count of Hinsdale. It was a hereditary title. The Crown giveth and the Crown taketh, I was demoted to the Baron of Hinsdale.

"As a hereditary peer, I attended the House of Lords a few times, an institution that needs to be abolished. The only notable memory I have is meeting one of Isabel's admirers in Parliament's private restaurant. Five years or so ago. He was with a new member of Parliament, a paki from Leeds, I think."

22

"Do you remember the MP's name?" I asked.

"Afram Gurmani."

7 Karen

As we left Grantchester, Harold was on his phone with his team. "Isabell attended *The Hermitage* in York. It is a boarding school for troubled girls. Probably sometime between 2010 and 2015. Her mother said she was close friends with Karen Wilson. …. No, I don't know where we can find her. I want you to contact the school and get the Wilson's address and any information you can on Karen."

Harold then went quiet and listened to the team leader. Disconnecting, he said, "We may have found a lead in Soho. The bartender at the *Shady Bitch*, a lesbian hangout, said there was a man Isabell claimed was following her. He's an occasional customer. My people are tracking him down."

"Tomorrow's Tabloid headline," said Harold, "Beautiful Royal lesbian stalked by straight male found strangled in the alley may not be far from the truth. No international intrigue for you to solve George."

"If only so simple," I said. "But we have other leads to run to ground."

The following morning, Harold's team leader reported that they had found the Wilsons. Mr. Wilson owned a small factory that made specialized parts for North Sea drilling rigs. They were estranged from their daughter but did have her last address in Glasgow.

Some online research found that Karen was an active supporter of the pro-independence Scottish National Party. Great, I'm thinking, I've been down this road before.

"Are you up for a trip to Glasgow?" asked Harold. We have tickets for the early morning flight. We might be able to do this in one day, but pack an overnight bag."

Glasgow was as gloomy as I remembered, a continual state of drizzle. We found Karen at the SNP headquarters. After brief introductions, Harold asked if there was a place we could talk privately.

"There's a wee tea shop next door. It should be empty this time of day," Karen said.

I ordered us a pot of tea, disgusting stuff, and some pastries as we gathered around a small table.

"We understand you and Isabell were close friends at *The Hermitage*," Harold said.

"That was a dreadful place; I'll never forgive my parents for sending me there. Isabell felt the same way. We retreated into our own world, a world the staff couldn't get into. When we were 'released,' and yes, I mean released, the place was a prison; we promised to stay in touch. I visited her a couple of times in London before I joined the SNP and moved here. Then we drifted apart."

"Did you know Isabell has been murdered?" I asked.

Karen's face drained of blood. She gulped some tea and asked, "When?"

"About three weeks ago," responded Harold.

"Do you know anyone who would want her dead?" I asked.

"Her parents," whispered Karen. In a louder voice, "No."

We talked a bit more with Karen and of what she remembered of Isabell, probing for other leads. Harold told her of the *Shady Bitch*.

"You think she was a lesbian?" smiled Karen. "She was into boys. If they wore pants, she'd try to seduce them. In her second year, she got one of the ground keepers fired when his son was found doing it with her in the bushes."

"The New Caledonian Order of Scotland," I said, "what does that mean to you?"

Karen looks at me with some puzzlement. "What does that have to do with Isabell? They are a right-wing group that advocates for Scotland's independence, by armed force if necessary. Two years ago, their leadership was massacred after being accused of assassinating Lord Ashford. Ashford was a strong spokesman for a united United Kingdom. The SNP has very little to do with the NCOS."

"But there is some interaction between the two," I said overly aggressively.

Somewhat taken aback by my attack, "Yes," Karen admitted.

***

It was a one day visit. On the plane back to London, I asked Harold what he thought.

"I don't think there is anything there."

"My sense is there is something she is not telling us," I said. "It's obvious she was shocked on learning of Isabell's death, but..."

The team had been busy. When we got back to the MET we found they had brought a Gordy Howard in for questioning. He was, supposedly, Isabell's stalker, a charge he vehemently denied.

8 Gordy

"Tell us about Isabell?" said DI Lynn.

We were sitting in one of the MET's interview rooms. Harold allowed me in the room, somewhat against procedure. "You are here to observe," he said. "I'll do the questioning.

"She was a flirt that hung out at some of the bars," Gordy said.

"Did you ever get together with her?"

"No, she hardly gave me the time of day."

"That's not what we've been told. You were seen frequently in her company. And leaving the *Shady Bitch* together on several occasions. Where did you go?"

"To get coffee."

"Come Gordy, you can do better than that," said Harold.

"Look, that's all; we were just casual friends."

"You know your apartment was searched after you were picked up last night. Guess what we found?"

The poor guy was left sitting there with a puzzled look on his face. "What?"

"A lady's scarf."

"So, that could have been anyones. It was probably Lucy's."

Harold, looking at him, shakes his head. "We are having the scarf checked for Isabell's DNA. It will be easier on you if you come clean now," he said.

Gordy slumps in his chair. "Okay, it was Isabell's. She was with me for an hour or so. She came by to get 'serviced.' That's all I was to her. Someone to screw when she got horny."

"What night was that Gordy," I asked.

DI Lynn gave me a sharp look, "answer him!"

"A Friday night about three weeks ago."

"That's a rather shaky alibi," said Harold. Can anyone corroborate your tale?"

Looking at Harold, Gordy says, "Talk with Francis. She's in tight with Isabell. She is a regular at the *Shady Bitch*; she was always teasing me about being Isabell's toyboy."

"Isabell mentioned something about a busy weekend she had planned with some dude."

"Who?" asked Harold.

"She never said."

Stepping into the hallway, Harold asks, "What do you think?"

"It's strange enough to be true," I said. "Who's the dude she was going to meet?"

My last comment was said to Harold's back. He had turned to the desk sergeant, "Bring in Francis. The bimbo can probably be found at the *Shady Bitch*."

We were back in the integration room at eleven that night. Francis sitting across the table from us.

"Do you know Gordy Howard?" asked Harold.

"Ya, that little weasel Isabell was stringing on."

28

"What do you mean stringing on?"

Looking somewhat embarrassed, Francis said, "She used him to get 'it' whenever the urge hit, but she would never be seen on the street with him."

"Three weeks ago, on a Friday night, Gordy claims he serviced Isabell. She mentioned something about a busy weekend she had planned with some dude. Any idea who this dude might be?"

"No. ... Wait, she was bragging she had a weekend planned with an older gentleman, a member of Parliament."

"Did this gentleman have a name?" asked Harold.

"It was funny sounding name, a foreigner."

"Afram Gurmani," said Harold.

Surprised, Francis answered, "Yes, that's it. How did you know?"

9 Afram Gurmani

"Have your people had any luck in finding Afram Gurmani?" I asked.

"No. His people in Westminster have no idea where he is. He left the office three weeks ago and has not been seen since. His constituency is in Leeds. We've contacted the local constabulary, asking for their assistance in locating Mr. Gurmani. He hasn't been seen there in six months."

"Would you mind if I went up there and knocked on a few doors?" I asked.

"No, that's probably a good idea. I'll call ahead and ask the locals to give you a hand," said Harold.

The following morning, and a short flight north, I was met at Leeds airport by Sargent Baldwin, a rotund man in his late forties with thinning hair but made up for with a luxurious handlebar mustache.

"Mr. Basdakis, I'm Sargent Baldwin. DI Lynn asked me to look after you. Said you wanted information on our MP, Afram Gurmani."

"Thanks for meeting me Sargent. Where do you think we should start looking?"

"Well, if it were my choice, I'd start with his parents."

"Yes, a good starting point. Do you have a car, or should I get a rental?"

"I've got one of the department's if that suits you, sir."

"That works for me, and please call me George. Let's go."

"Yes sir," Baldwin said as he led me to an unmarked police sedan."

Twenty minutes later, we were pulling up to a well-kept bungalow with rose bushes in the front. Red roses to the left of the walkway and white to the right.

"As you can see, they are nonpartisan," said a smiling Baldwin.

It was clearly an immigrant neighborhood, Pakistani I'm guessing. Baldwin rang the bell; a moment later, an elderly lady in a traditional *shalwar kameez* opened the door. I introduced myself. She invited us in and, as hospitality dictated, offered us tea. I declined, asking her not to go to any trouble on our behalf.

Her husband joined us. After Baldwin told him we were looking for their son, Afram. They both became not hostile but less than friendly. "We haven't seen him in weeks," the old man said.

"Has he called you?" I asked.

"No."

"Do you have any idea where he might be?"

"London," he said.

"Afram sponsored our immigration to the UK five years ago," the mother said. "We don't leave the local community much and have no idea where he might be if not in his office."

As we drove away, Sargent Baldwin said. "That went better than I expected. There is a fair amount of friction between the Pakistani community and the police."

"There is a large Pakistani community in Leeds; most arriving in the UK since the 1960s. With some exceptions, they are a pretty self-contained community. The major problem is the skinheads that

31

assault paki shop owners. The owners can't or won't identify the assailants, and the community blames the police for not arresting the assailants."

Does Afram Gurmani have a local political headquarters?" I asked.

"Just off Middleton Grove Road by the sports center," Baldwin answered. "Our next stop?"

"Yup."

Afram Gurmani's local headquarters was a storefront with a poster in the window identifying Afram Gurmani as 'Your Local MP;' with the message, COME IN AND LET'S CHAT.

We found a young man behind the reception desk, deeply engrossed with a video game. If we didn't speak, he may have missed us.

"When will Mr. Gurmani be in?" I asked. Other than the washroom in the back, it was a one-room affair.

Somewhat perturbed, he looked up, "Not today," he replied.

"I asked when!"

Sargent Balwin, displaying his police credentials, suggesting, "We could talk at the local station."

We had the young man's attention. It turned out he was a student, hired part-time to man the desk. He said he'd go days with no visitors. He had never met the MP and had no idea when he'd be in.

"Okay, you know nothing. Who does?" I aggressively said.

The young man fumbled in the back of the desk and came up with a worn business card. "Mr. Jabaal."

The card listed Mr. Jabaal's address in the city's industrial area and had a phone number.

"Should we call first," Baldwin asked.

"No, a surprise visit might work better."

We found Jabaal's office in the back of an old warehouse. Three toughs were reluctant to let us in. After a quick tussle, I had two on the ground and Baldwin restraining the third.

"Okay take us to Mr. Jabaal," Baldwin said as he held the tough's arm behind his back, feet inches off the floor.

Jabaal's office contrasted sharply with the shoddy warehouse. It was a Victorian office complete with plants.

Jabaal was a Pakistani in his late 50s. Skinny, a full head of black hair, and a sour expression. He could have been a villain in a B B-rated movie.

After thanking Jabaal's 'receptionist,' we seated ourselves, uninvitedly, on two antique overstuffed chairs.

Mr. Jabaal," I started, "we are looking for Afram Gurmani. We were directed here by a young man at Mr. Gurmani's constituent's headquarters. He could not help us and pointed to you. Our reception by your three men is troubling. What are you hiding?"

"And who the hell are you," he snapped.

"George Basdakis, with MI-5," I said, showing him the credentials Milo had given me just for an occasion like this. "If you like, I can get Scotland Yard up here to open an inquiry."

"As I just said, we are looking for Afram Gurmani, a Parliament member who appears to be missing."

"I'm Mr. Gurmani's campaign manager. I haven't seen him in over a month."

"Any idea where he might be?" I asked.

"No."

As Baldwin and I left Jabaal's warehouse. "That was unproductive," he said.

"You think," I muttered as I called DI Lynn.

"Harold, what do you have on Jabaal Kambarzahi? He's **Afram Gurmani's campaign manager.** There is something not kosher here."

10 Karen's Story

As I was visiting Jabaal, Harold received an urgent call from Karen Wilson in Glasgow. She was in police custody after being found in the car of one of the New Caledonian Order of Scotland members on the Dumbarton docks. She was being charged with smuggling and possible terrorist activities.

I received Harold's call as Baldwin and I arrived back at the local police station.

"That was fast," I said; "what did you find on Jabaal?"

"I'm good but not that good. I just received a call from Karen Wilson," and he proceeded to give me the particulars.

Earlier that week Scottish authorities confiscated a shipment of American M4 carbines. The rifles were hidden in a shipment of cloth heading to the mills in Glasgow. The mills, a startup enterprise to reintroduce jobs to the area, were sponsored by the New Caledonian Order of Scotland. The Scottish Police Authority was tipped off by an anonymous call. The shipment was intercepted on the Dumbarton docks.

"She claims she was holding back when we talked with her about Isabell and may have information on the Order's activities. She will spill if we can help her."

"You're in Leeds; Glasgow is just up the road from you. Would you go up there and see what she has to say?"

I was a bit too quick in agreeing. Looking at a map, Glasgow was over 280 kilometers, as the crow flies, from Leeds, and I'm not a crow.

Timewise, it was a tossup between waiting for a flight and flying or driving. I opted to fly.

I found Glasgow's central police station and parked my rental in a visitor's space. Entering the lobby, I went to the desk sergeant and introduced myself, using the credentials Milo provided for the second time in two days.

"Mr. Basdakis, DI Lynn from Scotland Yard told us to expect you. Chief Inspector McDowell will be right down."

McDowell was a brute of a man, over six feet and a mass of muscle. He shook my hand; on the way to his office, I had time to pry my fingers apart.

"I understand you want to talk with Karen Wilson. I'm having her brought up to the interview room."

McDowell insisted on sitting in despite Karen's objections and threats not to talk.

"Karen, I'm here at your request," I said. "If you want my help, you'll have to talk; otherwise, I'm out of here."

"Earlier, you asked what connection the SND and the New Caledonian Order of Scotland had. I told you minimal. That's not quite true."

Okay, she said. McDowell has been in contact with Chief Inspector William Milne, my handler, and I've been given permission to tell you the full story, but it goes no further.

When I left school, the Police Service of Scotland recruited me. While attending their two-year course at the Scottish Police College, Milne took a special interest in me, more specifically in my abilities. He wanted to develop me for covert police assignments. I agreed, and that entailed an extra year of training with MI-5. My first field assignment was to join the SND at their request. The was a growing suspicion that some members were getting too close to the New Caledonian Order and other radical groups. I was to identify but not get involved. But...

Robbie got me involved with them last year."

"Who's Robbie?" I asked.

"He's my boyfriend—my former boyfriend! He introduced me to the Order's leaders last year, telling me they were looking for an SND contact to work with. I reported this to Chief Inspector Milne, and he encouraged me to go with it. They had been trying for years to get a person inside the New Caledonian Order.

"As things developed, I became more involved with their operation than intended, specifically smuggling weapons. They wanted a stash of weapons available to support an armed separation from the United Kingdom if necessary. They needed funding. I was asked to reach out to two of the minor Scottish National Party leaders who were thought to be sympathetic. They soundly rebuffed me, but later, one of them approached me and made a sizable personal donation. That donation funded the shipment which was just intercepted.

"Robbie and I were directed to coordinate with the weapons dealer. Most of this was done via the Internet, but we did meet briefly in Glasgow to make payment for the delivery, half up front, the other half on delivery."

Pulling out my cell, I pulled up a picture of Afram Gurmani. "Karen, do you recognize this man?" I asked.

She took my phone and studied the photo. "No. But the man in the background is the dealer who sold us the weapons."

Surprised, I retrieved my phone and took a second look at Gurmani's photo. In the background was Jabaal.

"Are you sure?" McDowell asked.

"I was sitting as close to him as I am to you," snapped Karen. "The bastard was putting the moves on me right in front of Robbie. I slapped him, and he almost throttled me before Robbie could pull him off."

Looking at Chief Inspector McDowell, "If you go to this farm," Karen was saying as she wrote down the location, "you will find a stockpile of weapons from previous shipments accumulated over the past several years. Chief Inspector Milne directed me to tell you about the weapons before they became a problem."

"You mentioned you had more information on Isabell; what?" I asked.

"During my last visit with her, she said she was shagging a paki MP, someone named Afram. He was from Leeds, but Isabell thought he was into other things. A few of his phone calls she eavesdropped on suggested smuggling."

Later, sitting in McDowell's office, McDowell said, "We arrested her to maintain her cover. Karen will be turned loose in the morning at Milne's request."

38

11 Murder

"I think we need to find this Gurmani character," I said to Harold. "Any luck in tracing him?"

"No. We sent a request to the Customs Office yesterday to see if there is any record of him leaving the country," he said. "But on a good note, here is the information you asked for on Jabaal."

"Jabaal emigrated to the UK from Pakistan ten years ago. And get this, his travel companion was Afram Gurmani, his cousin.

"For the past few years, Jabaal has been on Interpol's watch list for smuggling. Never caught red-handed, but he has been on the fringes of several smuggling operations. His associates in the UK are on the 'iffy' side, but he has not been tied to any crimes.

"Interpol thinks the rifles intercepted last week were shipped from Karachi. They intercepted calls between Jabaal and someone in Karachi, in code, believed to have been associated with that arms shipment. They've asked that we pick him up for questioning.

"Guess what? Jabaal is now reported missing," Harold said.

Harold continued, "Customs Agents backtracked the arms shipment to Liverpool, where it was offloaded from a container ship and placed on a coastal freighter. The container ship is owned by the Varun Shipping Company, which is based in Mumbi."

As we were sitting there, pondering our next move, my cell chirped. It was Chief Inspector McDowell. "Mr. Basdakis, I have bad news. Karan Wilson's body was found this morning in the River Clyde. She was strangled."

After a moment of stunned silence, "Any suspects?"

A wino on the riverside said he saw two men dump a body early yesterday. He couldn't identify them or the car, but he did recognize a sticker for the Leeds City Football Club on the rear of the car.

I disconnected.

"What was that about?" Harold asked.

I told him. "Karan's been murdered, and I think I know by who. Can you get a warrant to search Jabaal's warehouse in Leeds? Have Sargent Baldwin and a forensics team search any car they find there that has a Leeds City Football Club sticker on the back. They're looking for traces of Karan in the car or in the boot. And have him check the alibies the three toughs he and I met there when we visited."

12 Varun Shipping Company

"Rajee, how's the gemstone business? Ms. Woo confiscated my share of the business after the countercoup in Zimbabwe. She promised to continue sending my share of the profits to Saint Mary's Orphanage – claimed it was good for their image."

Rajee Gupta was the CEO of the Varun Shipping Company. He and I became acquainted after I discovered he had ordered the scuttling of the freighter, APJ Usha, and the subsequent insurance scam. After I had blackmailed him into making whole one of my clients, Dodekanisos Seaways, we entered into a tactical alliance.

In my off-hours, I'm the CEO of the Basdakis Shipping Brokerage Company. Maggie manages the company and is responsible for its success. I had a deal with Rajee for his assistance in Basdakis Shipping ventures in the Indian Ocean. In return, I would assist Varun Shipping in accessing Mediterranean ports.

Oh, the gemstone business, that was a small operation Bhekizulu, Zimbabwe's Minister of Resources initiated. A clandestine operation harvesting river gravel rich in gemstones. My role was the middleman between Bhekizulu and Rajee. The gravel was shipped to Mumbai where it was auctioned off to the city's gem dealers. As an ongoing business, it made modest profits for all involved. Bhekizulu directed his share to go into supporting his country's numerous orphanages. Guilt caused me to do the same.

"Rajee, I didn't call to chitchat; British authorities have tracked arms being smuggled into Scotland. The shipment of the container moving the contraband originated in Karachi. It was carried by the SS Firoza, one of your freighters I believe."

"I'm not an arms dealer," snapped Rajee. "That could get my ships confiscated!"

"No one is saying you are. The weapons, not a large stash, were hidden in a shipment of cloth being shipped to Glasgow. We are trying to backtrack that shipment. Who shipped it? Where did the weapons come from? The shipping container's ID is XTG U 721756 9. Documentation indicates the container left Karachi three months ago.

"Here is a picture of two of our suspects," I said as I uploaded Jabaal's and Afram's photos, sending it to Rajee. The photos are of two Pakistanis, one named Jabaal Kambarzahi and the other Afram Gurmani. Would you ask your people in Karachi if they've seen either or have heard their names?"

"Let me look into this," said Rajee.

He continued, "How are you involved with this? The CEO of a Greek company, a dealer in questionable gems, a blackmailer, now you are an international agent?

"Something like that, we'll talk later," and I disconnected.

13 Recap

Commander Milo scheduled a meeting at 0800 hours to discuss the status of our investigation into Isabell's murder. I arrived a bit early, wanting the first crack at the coffee pot.

When would I learn, coffee was a secondary stimulant for the British, tea was the preferred beverage? Fortunately, I had time to get a large coffee at Starbucks. Starbucks had the franchise in the building's lobby.

By the time I got back to the conference room, they had started. "It's nice that you can join us," Milo said.

Sitting around the table was Commander Milo from MI-5; Detective Chief Inspector Allenby and Detective Inspector Harold Lynn, both from Scotland Yard; and, to my surprise, Sir Charles from MI-6.

Harold started with a recap of the case. "We found that Isabell was in a sexual relationship with Afram Gurmani, a member of Parliament. He is her senior by twenty years. Gurmani was born in Pakistan and was granted British citizenship eighteen years ago. It was reported by Karen, I'll get to her in a minute, that Isabell overheard several telephone conversations between Gurmani and an unknown person that may have dealt with a supposed smuggling operation."

Commander Milo asked, "Have you interviewed Gurmani?"

"No, we can't find him," said Harold.

"We also talked with Gordy Howard," continued Harold. "He also had a sexual relationship with Isabell. Isabell was the dominant partner and had threatened to end the relationship several times. It appears that the relationship was for her convenience; Isabell's friends at the *Shady Bitch* referred to him as her 'toy boy.'

"This brings me to Karen Wilson. Karen was a close school friend of Isabell and is the person providing the details between Isabell and Gurmani. Karen, a member of the Scottish National Party, was recently recruited by the New Caledonian Order of Scotland and is privy to the Order's importation of smuggled arms. She was also working with the police authorities in Glasgow as an undercover agent. A busy girl.

"Karen was murdered, her body dumped in the River Clyde. We believe Jabaal Kambarzahi ordered her murder. He is the smuggler of the weapons intercepted at Dundee. Karen was going to testify to that. Now, the interesting piece. Kambarzahi and Gurmani are cousins, immigrating to the UK together twenty years ago. Jabaal is also missing."

"A quick recap," said Milo, "has Gurmani suspected of Isabell's murder, but there is no evidence supporting this. Kambarzahi is suspected of ordering Karen's murder, but there is no evidence supporting this either. And both Gurmani and Kambarzahi cannot be found."

Somewhat sheepishly, Chief Inspector Allenby nodded his agreement.

Sir Charles cleared his throat and started with, "I may have something to add. The two dozen M4 carbines intercepted in Dundee, and using their serial numbers, we were able to trace them to Afghanistan ... where they were left by the US last year."

Not to be left out, I added, "These weapons were shipped from Karachi on the SS Firoza, a freighter owned by the Varun Shipping Company. I've spoken with the CEO, and he is looking for details on this shipment."

Sir Charles, looking a bit miffed by the interruption, continued, "The stockpile of weapons Karen identified contained a variety of assault rifles: M4s, M16s, and AK47s. We think these were purchased in small batches from weapon dealers over the past several years. Many of the M4s and M16s were reported stolen; as for the AKs, god only knows where they came from."

"We are working with the Greek Intelligence Service to identify weapon dealers. One of the suspected dealers, but we have no evidence of his involvement, is Isabell's uncle, Amal Choucair. He lives in Beirut. He also makes frequent visits to England to visit family." Looking at Commander Milo, Perhaps he should be interviewed."

14 Matchmaker

Our flight to Beirut had a stopover in Athens. I convinced Harold that we needed to extend our time in Athens. I needed to talk to Uncle Alexander and see what he knew about Amal Choucair and his smuggling network. I also wanted a little time with Maggie.

In the airport arrival area, I called Maggie, asking if she could fly to Athens for the weekend. Then, not being able to reach Alexander, I called Kostas Doukas, Alexander's up-and-coming spook.

"Mr. Basdakis will be in the office by the time we get there. He was sleeping in late this morning," said Kostas as we got into the GIS limousine.

"Harold, this is Kostas Doukas, one of Alexander's new spooks. He rescued me in Singapore last year. Kostas. This is Detective Inspector Harold Lynn from Scotland Yard. We are working together to track down the person who murdered my cousin."

"Your uncle said you were in England but didn't provide any details."

"Need to know," I said.

Walking into the Greek Intelligence Service's inner lair, we were passing the Director's office just as the door opened and Constance stepped into the hallway.

"George, I wasn't expecting to see you; you are supposed to be in the UK. Who is your friend?"

"Ms. Gabris, I was, but now we are on our way to Beirut to chase a lead. This is Detective Inspector Harold Lynn from Scotland Yard. Harold, this is my boss, Constance Gabris, Director of the Greek Intelligence Service. I'm here to pick my uncle's memory about an arms smuggler."

"That old goat, he's forgotten more than we will ever know. I think he's in his office," she said as she headed down the hall.

We found Alexander in his office waiting for us. After introductions, I got to the point. "What can you tell us about Amal Choucair, Isabell's Lebanese uncle?"

"He runs an import/export company and occasionally deals in smuggled weapons. He works out of Beirut but has or had offices in other major cities. Last I heard, he is mostly retired, occasionally dabbling in the trade a bit. Why?"

"It concerns Isabell's murder. He is not suspected of being involved, but there are several questions he can help us with. We want to talk with him."

After a bit more talk, Alexander agreed to arrange a meeting with Amal Choucair for us.

I declined Alexander's offer to put us up for the night in his modest fifteen-room estate on the waterfront. "Thanks, but MI-5 is funding this trip," I said.

We checked into a downtown hotel. Maggie was already there. "You said you were with a Scotland Yard detective," she said, "but you didn't mention he was young and attractive—unattached, I hope. I invited Elena to join us for dinner."

Maggie had made dinner reservations for us at one of Athens' more exclusive restaurants, one her father owned.

47

Maggie's father was known to dabble in the black market. He owned several bars in addition to this restaurant. A few years ago, I introduced him to an old Brazilian business partner from my past. Gustaf had fled South America when the local police came after him. He claimed I ratted him out. In truth, his goose was cooked before I gave my statement. Maggie's father and Gustaf got into a car export business, stolen cars going from Europe to North Africa.

We were just being seated on the patio when Elena arrived.

"Elena, this is Harold," I said. "He's a detective with Scotland Yard. Harold, this is Elena, Maggie's close friend and the widow of my cousin."

We had a very pleasant evening. Demetri, Maggie's father, made it a point to have a full bottle of wine on our table. Later that night, back at the hotel, Maggie commented, "Elena and Harold appeared to enjoy each other's company."

"Maggie, no matchmaking, please. We're here on serious business."

The next morning Harold was still captivated by Elena. "Is she seeing anyone?" he asked.

I looked at him, "Run," I said. "Maggie is playing matchmaker, and you are in her sights. If you get involved with a Greek woman, she will own your private life."

15 Amal Choucair

We arrived at Beirut International Airport early the next afternoon. Approaching the city from the air, I could see two columns of smoke from the city's center.

Amal Choucair had two of his men meet us in a black Mercedes-Maybach. "Mr. Choucair told us to take you to his home. You will be staying there. It's safer."

"What was that smoke I saw in the center of the city as we landed?" I asked.

"One of the local political factions trying to make a point, or it could have been the Israelis taking out a Hezbollah leader. Who knows these days," the driver said with some resignation.

Amal's home was north of the city in the Lebanese foothills. The Mediterranean was just visible on the horizon. Did I say home? It was an estate that rivaled my uncle's.

A portly man greeted us. "You must be George, Alexander's nephew." Turning to Harold, "And I believe you are Detective Inspector Harold Lynn."

"George, it's nice to meet you. Your uncle and I have been playing cat 'n mouse for the past three decades. He's good, but I've always stayed a step or two in front."

49

"I've had two rooms made up for you: much more pleasant than staying in a hotel. My staff will take your bags while we have a cool drink by the pool."

The pool, not as large as an Olympic size pool, was kidney-shaped with a bevy of young people. "My grandchildren and their friends," he said. Let's use the table over there under the trees; it's more private."

As we sat, the pool attendant brought over a tray of glasses, iced tea, and some snacks.

"It's much more pleasant here than in my office. Now, what can I do for you?"

"We want to talk about Isabell," I started. "I'm sure by now Nadine, your niece, has told you of her death."

"Yes, I still can't accept it," he said, a tear coming to his eye. "We were close, closer than she was with her parents."

"Did Nadine tell you Isabell was murdered?"

"NO!"

"She was strangled three weeks ago, this past Saturday. Her body was found dumped in an alley."

"We are treating this conversation as a formal interview for our investigation. Inspector Lynn will be taping it," I said as Harold turned on the record app on his phone. "What can you tell us about Isabell?"

In the past thirty seconds, Amal looked as if he'd aged ten years. "I was always close to Isabell. She was a precious child. As she got older, a more rebellious age, her parents were losing control and placed her in an all-girls boarding school, in York I believe. I saw her a few times when she was home. She hated that school. Claimed to have only one friend there."

"Karen Willson?" I said.

"Yes. They were close."

"When Isabell was almost eighteen, she left school, ran away really. Went to London and fell in with some shady people. I tried to convince her to go home; her parents were worried about her, and I was worried about her. She refused, so I rented her a flat. Couldn't have here living on the street could I? I also gave her a small stipend to cover living expenses. This went on for a few years. She hung out at some lesbian lounge, claiming she liked the people; they were nonjudgmental. No, she wasn't homosexual; she liked men, probably liked them too much."

"Who killed her?" Amal demanded.

Ignoring his question, "Karen Wilson was also murdered," I said and recounted the events leading to her death.

"What does all that have to do with Isabell's murder," snapped Amal.

"The person who ordered Karen's death was Jabaal Kambarzahi. He is the arms dealer who was supplying the New Caledonian Order of Scotland with the weapons."

"Have you ever heard of him?" I asked as I showed him Jabaal's picture.

"No, I've stepped back from the trade," he said with some defiance.

"Isabell was having an affair with Afram Gurmani, twenty years her senior and a member of Parliament. Isabell confided with Karen that she overheard Gurmani talking with someone about a smuggling operation. She snooped a bit and discovered he was involved with a black market weapons dealer, possibly Jabaal."

"And Afram Gurmani, is that a name familiar to you?" I asked as I showed him the next picture.

"No."

"Kambarzahi and Gurmani are cousins. They immigrated together to the UK together twenty years ago."

"We think Gurmani found out Isabell was eavesdropping on his calls and killed her."

Amal's face was now one of rage, "WHERE CAN I FIND THESE BASTARDS?"

Before responding, I asked Harold to stop the recording. "I wish we knew; both have disappeared," I said. "They are Pakistani; the intercepted weapons were shipped from Karachi. I'd start there."

"I need to digest all this," said Amal as he waived the attendant over. Please take my guest to their rooms; they might want to freshen up."

Looking at us, "We can continue our conversation later. I was planning dinner, but maybe we will just have a snack in my study."

As we entered my room, Harold said agitatedly, "What were you thinking? Telling him who our suspects are and where to find them?"

"And we are going to do what? Go into Pakistan's underworld and extract two felons?" I responded. "If it were a national security issue, Sir Charles might. But for simple murder, us, not a chance. Now, on the other hand, Amal will have access to people who can eliminate Gurmani and Kambarzahi. And, you will have to agree, is a measure of justice."

***

Amal had sandwiches served in his study. "Would you care for a beer with that?" Amal asked. "I'm just having tea."

"Tea is fine," we said in unison.

"I appreciate what you have shared with me," said Amal. I know it was against protocol. I also suspect you shared the information with me knowing it would be impossible for British authorities to extract Gurmani and Kambarzahi from Pakistan—and that I could."

52

"Let me share with you some information I have," said Amal. It is rumored that there will be a large shipment of arms, most coming from Afghanistan, going to rebels in Djibouti. This shipment is expected sometime in the next three months. And no. I don't know who. My normal rivals are not involved. The operation may be state-sponsored. **Gurmani** and Kambarzahi may be involved."

"As you may know, Djibouti's government is holding on by a thread. The county hosts the American base, **Camp Lemonnier**, that flies most of the large weapon-carrying drones in the Mideast. The Chinese also have a base there. As you can imagine, there is a level of tension between the two. If the rebels succeed, Djibouti will become another Somalia."

"Please pass this information along to Alexander. He and his MI-6 friends will find it interesting but do not mention my name. If it gets out that I leaked the information, I'm a dead man."

16 The Choucair Clan

The following morning, before we left, Amal gave us his family's recent history over breakfast.

"After World War I, Leabon was in shambles, people starving on the streets. The French provided some aid, but not enough. My father and grandfather had a trading company, a dockside warehouse, and three small coastal freighters. They brought in grain from Egypt making the Choucair Trading Company one of the most prosperous in Beirut.

"The French Commandant's demand for bribes became excessive. My father started smuggling weapons for the local resistance.

"Lebanon was then administered by a League of Nations Mandate. As armed resistance grew, the Mandate's leaders were wise enough to remove the French Commandant. All was good, but...

"Now, I'm sure you know some of Palestine's history. As word spread between resistance leaders that the Choucair Trading Company was a good source for smuggled weapons, my father became a major weapons dealer in the Levant.

"My grandfather played cat 'n mouse with Field Marshal Allenby in the early 20s. Allenby the cat, my grandfather the mouse. Allenby's people almost nabbed my grandfather's vessels twice with a load of smuggled weapons. The thing that saved him was the ongoing animosity between the French and the British. Authorities in Beirut were loath to turn any of its citizens over to the British.

"When my father retired in the '70s, I took over the operation.

"The first Palestinian Intifada in the late 80s resulted in a new influx of Palestinian refugees and the establishment of Hezbollah in the refugee camps. Terrorist attacks on Israel and Israeli counterstrikes made Beirut a dangerous place to live. My father was killed in the '90s when Israel invaded Lebanon—killed by Hezbollah gunfire. I moved my mother and younger sister to Marseilles.

"My sister was in her late 20s when she met Rupert, an English playboy. I was on the verge of removing him when Nadine told me to leave him alone or she'd have my nuts. They got married, and Isabel was born.

"Isabel was the shining light in my life. Afram Gurmani is a dead man. The only question is, how does he die?"

17 The Professor

After fleeing London, Afram Gurmani made his way to Pakistan via less traveled roads. In Karachi, he found refuge with some of his old smuggling associates. Two weeks after arriving, who shows up? Jabaal Kambarzahi.

"That was the dumbest thing you ever did," said Jabaal, "killing that girl. It's not something that, as your campaign manager, would have recommended. You were in the British Parliament, on various committees having access to information that is critical to our operation. Now what? You're wanted by Interpol for murder."

"And you," shot back Afram, "ordering that murder in Scotland!"

Jabaal cracks a smile, "I guess we both screwed up. What are your immediate plans?

"We have a cousin in Peshawar who is a professor at the Farabi Degree College. He's invited me to conduct a short course on the British parliamentary system this coming term," said Afram.

A few days later, Jabaal and Afram are back in the tea house plotting. "Are you still going to Peshawar?" asked Jabaal.

"Yes."

"Good, that's not far from Kabul, where there is an abundance of American weapons. A Chinese operative has approached me about securing some of these weapons. The Chinese consulate in Kabul assures her that the Taliban is eager to make a sale. What we need is a man in Kabul to assist her in selecting weapons and preparing them for transport to a freighter. This is a job you are well qualified for. Interested?"

With a puzzled look, Afram says, "You keep saying her. Who is 'her' and what does she know about illicit arms sales?"

"Madam Woo. She's a legend. She's brought down more than one government. I'll contact you when you get to Peshawar and provide meeting information for you and Madam Woo in Kabal."

***

A week later, Afram's cousin sets up a meeting with the college's Dean of Political Studies. "I see here Professor Gurmani has recommended you as an instructor for our upcoming spring course on the British parliamentary system. One question, if you don't mind, what qualifies you?"

"I was a member of Parliament for five years, representing Leeds."

Somewhat surprised, the Dean asks," Why did you leave?"

"A conflict in cultural values," said Afram.

Three weeks later, Jabaal notified Afram of the arranged Kabal meeting. The timing was great; the college was closed for ten days, three to repair a plumbing problem and seven for a State holiday celebrating a recent election victory.

Kabal was an all-day bus ride. In a civilized country, it should have been no more than two hours. But be it as it may, he arrived in the early evening and checked into the hotel that Jabaal recommended.

Early the next morning his cell was ringing. "Meet me in the lobby in thirty minutes," said a no-nonsense female voice in impeccable English.

Afram was ten minutes early, leaving enough time to find tea, his morning wake-up beverage.

57

An attractive thirtyish Asian lady sat down across from him, "Afram Gurmani?" she asked.

"Yes, and you are Madam Woo. I've heard a lot about you. Single-handedly taking over the Zimbabwean lithium mines."

"Don't believe everything you hear," she said. You're here to help me select weapons and prepare them for shipment. Here is my 'want' list; probably more than we can get or ship, but it is a starting point."

After a quick glance, "Who's paying for this?" he asks.

"Not your concern. We have an appointment in two hours with Mohammad Yaqoob, the Defense Minister."

As they were ushered into Yaqoob's office, Afram saw a man who was several years his junior. Getting up, he asked if they would like tea. Tea was mandatory prior to any serious discussions. Tea was served, and after some small talk, Mohammad got to the point.

"You want American weapons; we want to sell you those weapons. How are you going to pay?"

"My government will pay," said Woo. "Payment will include shipment. My man here will coordinate with your people."

Well, let's see what you are buying. I will have my assistant take you to Bagram Air Base where the weapons are stored. You select what you need, and we will talk later.

Once Madam Woo selected her items and negotiated the final price with Mohammad: one-half of the sale price now, the balance when the shipment arrived at Pishukan. She left town, leaving Afram to work with the locals to prepare the weapons for shipment.

18 Intelligence

I opted to return to England via Greece. Not for Harold's sake, although he was happy with the stop in Athens, I wanted to consult with my uncle.

This time, we stayed at his home; it would be a short visit. That afternoon, we told Alexander about the pending arms deal that Amal had told us about.

"That sounds like a major operation," he said. I've heard nothing about it from my grapevine. You say this shipment is expected sometime in the next three months."

"What does your friend in Mumbi know?" he asked. "Call him while I set up a secure conference call with Sir Charles and his American counterpart."

Stepping out of the room, I hit Rajee's number; I now had it on speed dial.

"Rajee, it's George. Quick question: Have you heard anything about a large weapons shipment going to Djibouti from Karachi or any other port? It's supposedly scheduled for sometime in the next three months."

"George, you think I'm a weapons dealer or knowingly deal with those people? As one of your famous TV characters was fond of saying, "I know nothinggggg."

59

"Seriously, I have heard no rumors that hint a shipment like this. But, and this is just a wild thought, one of my Captains mentioned last month he saw an old freighter, the Al Murtaza Ali. He thought the ship had gone to the scrapyard, but it was docked in Pishukan, a small backwater town in western Pakistan near the Iranian border, where it was being worked on. He wondered why anyone would be putting money into that bucket of rust. Now, my thought is, what better way to smuggle a large shipment of weapons than on an unregistered ship?"

"To further my theory, Pishukan is only five hundred kilometers from Djibouti, only a day away, and is linked by major roads to Kandahar. Smuggling is a way of life in Baluchistan."

"Okay Rajee, thanks. I owe you," I said as I was digesting what he had just told me and resumed my seat at the conference table.

Alexander had Sir Charles and John Holland, the CIA Assistant Director for Seaborn Threats, on the wall-mounted split screen when I returned. Harold was just finishing recounting Amal's information.

"George, did Rajee have any information?" Alexander asked.

"Nothing concrete, but he did have an interesting theory. An old, decommissioned freighter, the Al Murtaza Ali, built in 1942, is being worked on in the port of Pishukan. Pishukan is only a day's sail from Djibouti ... and it is connected to Kandahar by paved roads. Rajee thought, what better way to smuggle weapons than by an unregistered freighter?"

I had Sir Charles and John Holland's attention.

"I'll have our people put a satellite on it to monitor the ship's movements. Good call, but I have to go now," said Holland, and with that, the American feed went dead.

"A real Schmuck!" said Sir Charles. "He's probably in his boss's office by now, claiming credit for uncovering this threat and proposing a solution. Unfortunately, I have to deal with him."

Directed to Harlod and me, Sir Charles asked, "Can you catch the evening's flight back to London?"

Harold quickly turned to me, giving me the eye, as he said, "No sir, we still have one or two loose ends to chase down here."

After the call was terminated, Alexander turned to me, "Loose ends?"

"Harold has a date with Elena," I said with a smile. "Maggie's matchmaking efforts are paying off."

19 Camp Lemonnier

By the time we got back to London, Scotland Yard had issued arrest warrants for Jabaal Kambarzahi and Afram Gurmani for the murders of Karen Wilson and Isabel Windsor, respectively. At what I thought was our last team meeting, I suggested it was time I drop off the team; my work was done.

"Done. You've just started," said Sir Charles. "You and Harold uncovered a possible major weapons smuggling operation. Kambarzahi and Gurmani are still missing. There is a strong possibility one or both are involved. No my boy, you are still part of the team."

Commander Milo added, "We've been talking and think it might be a good idea if we got ahead of this shipment by sending you two to Djibouti to coordinate with the local authorities."

"Djibouti, no way," said Harold. "I work for Scotland Yard and besides, I have no authority there."

"Not a problem," said Detective Chief Inspector Allenby. "The MET has transferred you to MI-6 for this operation. Sir Charles will see to your credentials."

Chuckling to myself, I turned to Harold, "Welcome to the world of spooks."

"I've been in contact with John Holland's assistant," said Sir Charles, "and am told NSA has eyes on the freighter. It is still moored at Pishukan. I am also trying to find you a CIA contact at Camp Lemonnier in Djibouti. And to brighten your day," continued Sir Charles, "you are both booked on a C-17 flying out of Rhein-Main Air Base. You have two days to get packed. An MI-6 Gulfstream will get you to Germany."

***

Harold and I were sitting in a row of passenger seats, obviously installed as an afterthought, in the Air Force Globemaster. There were thirty seats installed in the forward cargo bay, just behind the flight deck. The seats were installed backward; we faced the back of the plane, facing several hundred tons of cargo on palettes. Harold observed, "If we go down, that cargo will fly forward, squashing us like a bug."

There were seven military members flying Space-A and returning to duty at Camp Lemonnier. The one sitting closest to us heard Harold and piped up, "That's a blessing; you'll never know what hit you."

The flight lasted about eight hours. I slept most of the way. Midway the aircrew distributed box lunches. All things considered, the sandwiches weren't bad.

As we were disembarking, we were met by Dillon Rankin, the local CIA spook. Not to be obvious, he was the only person on the tarmac in civilian attire. "Welcome to Camp Lemonnier, the military's hidden resort, where it never rains, and the temperature is either hot or hotter. I've got you a couple of rooms at the BOQ. Let's get you settled in, and over a cold beer, you can tell me what's going on."

Dillion was a young man, probably just graduated from some Ivy League school and given three months of spook training by the CIA. Djibouti was most likely his first real assignment.

The Bachelor Officer Quarters were better than those that I remembered. The essential lounge was located on the backside of the first deck. There was a small patio area on the other side of the glass doors, which thankfully were shut; it was over a hundred degrees outside. It was late afternoon; the lounge was beginning to fill with other BOQ residents.

Dillon was waiting for us at a table in the back corner. "Okay, what brings you two to my little oasis? I was told to provide you assistance as needed, but nothing was said about your mission. So, what do you need?"

"I guess you have a need to know," said Harold. "We are here to intercept a freighter smuggling arms to the local rebels. We'll need your help when we take them down."

Growing a little alarmed, "You mean just the three of us?" said Dillon.

With a smile growing on his face, Harold added, "Is there a problem? There really is a freighter, but we are just here to observe. Our bosses will decide how to deal with it. Call in local authorities, an air strike, or insert a strike team to deal with them: decisions all above our pay grade."

"What we need now is an office with secure communications," I said. "We are not here for any heroics."

The next morning Dillon set us up in his office located in the back of an underutilized hangar. He also provided us with a vehicle to get around the camp, a Peugeot P4, left by the French.

20 Al Murtaza Ali

Dillon's communication equipment included the capability for a live NSA feed, which we tested. The Al Murtaza Ali was still at the Pishukan dock where we last saw her. It looks like there was activity on the dock; several trucks were queued up next to the freighter. "It looks like she's being loaded," said Dillon. Do you have any idea when she will set to sea, given she doesn't sink?"

"No, but it should be soon," I said.

There was a phone, an old landline unit sitting on Dillon's desk. "Does this antique still work?" I asked.

"Yes, and don't make fun of it; it's a state-of-the-art secure line."

"Can I call MI-6?" I was saying as I punched in Sir Charles's number.

His secretary answered on the second ring. "Is his lordship in?" I asked.

"Is that you, George? Your voice sounds a little high-pitched. I'll get him for you."

"I assume you are there. Good flight?" he said as he came on the line.

"Yes, we are here. It was an uneventful flight. I think commercial carriers have nothing to fear from the US Military Airlift Command. Our CIA contact is taking good care of us. Just calling to let you know we are here. Plan is, is to get a good night's sleep and see what tomorrow brings."

At five the next morning, Dillon was beating on my door. "The ship is gone."

Howard and I were gathered around the screen. The dock at Pishukan was empty. Moving further west, the NSA feed showed only a brown haze. "There is a massive sandstorm coming off the Arabian peninsula. Fine sand, up to a thousand feet, is masking visibility," said Dillion.

"What about the satellite's infrared abilities?" asked Harold.

"Only works for cloud cover," Dillion said.

"Can we get a drone in the air? We are north of the sandstorm. I want to see the ship when it reappears and where it is heading," I said with some urgency.

An hour later, Dillion had a drone flying over the Gulf of Aden where we picked up the Al Murtaza Ali just off the coast of Yemen, heading east at about twelve knots. We expected to see her take a southwest heading, taking her to Djibouti. Instead, she headed northwest into the Bab al-Mandab Strait.

"Where the hell is she going?" mumbled Harold.

An hour later, the satellite feed was re-established. The Al Murtaza Ali had left the Yemeni waters and was docking at what looked like an old oil offloading facility in Assab, a small village just on the other side of the Djibouti-Eritrea border.

"Dillion, how do we get up there?" I asked with some urgency. Not waiting for an answer, I studied the satellite images of the area. There were two roads going from Djibouti to Assab: a coastal road and an inland road. I could see no border crossing control points.

"Dillion, are these roads open between the two countries?"

66

"Yes," he answered, "only periodic roving patrols on the Eritrean side."

I gave Dillion a list of items we needed; Harold and I were going north.

Driving an old Suzuki SUV that Dillion was able to scrounge up, Peugeot was to iffy for a trip through the hinterlands, Harold and I headed north along the coastal highway. By eight that evening, we were registering at Assab's Kebal International Hotel. Not a fancy place, but one that could comfortably accommodate folks transiting the Red Sea.

21 Assab

The next morning, we did some scouting and found an excellent position on a hill overlooking the fuel storage area. It was secluded and provided an exceptional view of the dock … and of the Al Murtaza Ali. It appeared they were just starting to offload the cargo using the ship's crane, placing containers on a waiting flatbed truck.

Handing me the binoculars, Harold said, "Look at the man on the ship's flying bridge directing operations."

Taking the binoculars, I looked for the man Harold was pointing out. "That's Jabaal!"

No sooner than I recognized Jabaal, a rifle barrel, was prodding my back. Three men in military uniforms were in behind us. "What are you doing here?" asked one of them in good English who appeared to be in charge.

"Bird watching," said Harold.

As they bound our hands, the leader said with a smirk, "My captain will want to talk to you. Smart-ass answers will get you beaten."

He was right. After a couple of hours of interrogation, we were both bloody and on the verge of collapse. We were thrown into a cell at the back of the building—no water and no facilities, only a bucket and a single cot.

Other than the boy who gave us some bread and a bottle of putrid water, we saw no one for two days.

On the third day, Jabaal was not so gently put in the cell with us. At first, he didn't recognize me, but with a little prodding, I brought his memory back to Leeds.

After a few threats on my part to bust his ass and he confirmed he was smuggling weapons.

"I had a deal with the Chinese to smuggle weapons from Afghanistan to the rebels in Djibouti. The Chinese want to overthrow the government and close the American base. I was told the freighter was being redirected here, a better port to offload the cargo they said. All was going fine until this morning. Our deal was Eritrea would get some of our cargo; the rest would be smuggled into Djibouti. That little shit-eating captain told me his government had decided to keep all the weapons."

22 Surprise

After a surprisingly meager dinner, a middle-aged woman was put in our cell by smirking guards. "Have fun," they said mocking her.

After a flurry of Chinese that I'm sure was not complimentary, I recognized her – Ms. Woo. "Lynn, what are you doing here?"

Ignoring me, she turned on Jabaal. "You dog. You told them where I was. I told you not to worry; I'd get you out. But no, you tried to save your own ass! Now we're both in here."

Turning to me, "What the hell are you doing here?"

I gave her the Reader's Digest version summing it up with we were tracking the Al Murtaza Ali and the weapons shipment.

"MI-6?" she snapped, "my gut told me you were a spy when we first met."

My mind flashed back to that meeting in a hotel in Beira, Mozambique. I was on a mission for Sir Charles to monitor the Chinese as they worked to get control of the lithium mines in Zimbabwe.

"I have to congratulate your masters on a game well played. You now have control of Zimbabwe's lithium mines. But what do you want with Djibouti?"

"Simple, we want the Americans out."

"And you are going to do that from inside an Eritrea cell," I glibly said. "We have time; tell me the whole story."

"After our success in Zimbabwe, I was reassigned to the Djibouti desk," Lynn said. "The opposition party, *Front for the Restoration of Unity and Democracy,* yes, that is a mouth full so they go by the acronym FRUD, contacted Beijing looking for support to oust the clan who has an iron grip on the government. FRUD claims to have the backing of the common people but needs weapons."

"I called our consulate in Afghanistan to find a contact to make a deal for some of President Biden's abandoned arsenal. The American weapons were stored in a large hangar on the former Bagram Air Base. My Taliban tour guide took me to the hangar and told me to select what I wanted. A virtual K-Mart blue light sale! I was tempted by the Apache helicopters lined up on the tarmac but left with only a dozen pallets of assault rifles and RPGs and another dozen pallets with ammunition.

"Now, this was becoming a sizable shipment. My man in Karachi, this dog Jabaal, suggested I obtain an old freighter. He had a friend who was talking about scrapping an old rust bucket of a freighter, the Al Murtaza Ali. He would be willing to use it for a high-risk shipment if the price was right.

"Jabaal made arrangements to truck my cargo from Kandahar to Pishukan. Pishukan's attributes are that it is a small port that could make basic ship repairs, it was off the world's radar, and it was connected by a road network to Afghanistan. I was impressed.

"Chinese intelligence agencies knew that their counterparts in the West were onto my plan, so when that dust storm came along, we took full advantage of it. We followed the coastline for the next twelve hours. As we neared Aden, I directed the ship into the Bab al-Mandab Strait with Assab being our new destination. My people in

Beijing assured me that the Eritreans were fully on board with this. Payment: 10 percent of our shipment.

"All was going fine. Jabaal was offloading our shipment onto flatbed trucks, which the Eritreans had provided. Then that ^#*%$@," a Chinese curse words I've never heard before, "told me his government had decided to keep the entire shipment and I would be held until a ransom was paid."

"The fool took me but confined my men to the freighter."

"That's an interesting story, but on a more urgent level, how are we going to get out of here?"

"Get some sleep; it's going to get interesting later tonight," she said.

***

I didn't get much sleep, drifted off a few times but never into what one would call sleep.

Sometime after midnight, all hell broke loose. Ms. Woo's people overwhelmed their guards on the freighter as Lynn knew they would, had taken the command headquarters with a barrage of small arms fire. One dragged a small man in uniform back and ordered him to open the cell. Once the cell door was open, he was shot. Stepping over the body, Lynn was yelling at us to move; we were leaving.

Outside her people had a large SUV they had commandeered, the captain's personal vehicle. "George, you drive; my people have a hard time staying on the road. Take the main road south."

Leaving Assab at a high speed, we crested the hill and could see the Djibouti foothills in the far distance. I could also see the three military vehicles closing fast. As they got closer, the more ambitious of the gunman started firing. They were still far enough behind us not to do any damage, discounting a lucky shot.

"Lynn, you wouldn't have a satellite phone, would you?" She reached into the bag one of her men brought and extracted the requested phone.

"Call this number and put the call on the speaker." After four rings Dillon answered.

"Dillon, where are you?"

"In my office, we've been trying to track you. The last we saw was you and Harold being escorted into a small block building south of Assab, close to where the Al Murtaza Ali is docked. That was three days ago."

I gave him a quick recap and asked if he still had eyes on us.

"I think so. An SUV just left that block house, and we think six or seven people got into it. It appears to be fleeing south with three vehicles chasing it."

"That's us. Is your drone armed?"

"Yes."

"Can you take out the vehicle directly behind us?"

The connection went silent, and a moment later, the lead pursuit vehicle was engulfed in a ball of flames.

"Does that help?" asked Dillion.

"Beautiful, we will be in downtown Djibouti in an hour or so. Maybe you can send someone to pick us up."

Lynn broke the connection and, looking at me, said, "And pick me up, too?"

"No, let's find a place between the Chinese Support Base and Camp Lemonnier and we can go our separate ways," I said.

We agreed that the Golden Airport Hotel on the outskirts of Djibouti was a good place to part company.

As we got out of the SUV, Harold and I grabbed Jabaal before he could make a run for it. "He's coming with us," I said.

"You're welcome to him," said Ms. Woo, "he's a liability."

"It's been fun George; let's hope we don't meet again," and with that, she and her crew disappeared into the hotel lobby.

23 Homebound

Our arrival back at Camp Lemonnier found Dillion under verbal attack by the Navy Command responsible for the smaller drones.

"Who the hell are you to authorize the release of ordnance in a neutral country?"

"What neutral country?" I said. "Eritrea is a coconspirator in a planned overthrow of a friendly government."

"And who the hell are you?" he yelled.

Taking my phone, I called Sir Charles. Putting him on the speaker, "Sir, I have an irate Navy Commander here who is looking for answers."

Having just been brought up to speed, Sir Charles said, "Commander, indulge me please, and hold the line for a minute."

A moment later, John Holland, the CIA Assistant Director, was speaking. After introductions, "Commander, I understand you have a problem. Do you want to discuss it? I was just speaking with SECNAV; I can call him back if you like."

The Commander's ego had just been deflated. "What can I do for you," he sheepishly asked me.

"We have a prisoner here," I said. "He's wanted for murder back in the UK. Would you hold him in the brig for us until we are ready to leave?"

Dillion arranged for us to fly Space-A to the Naval base at Rota, Spain. The flight was a MEDEVAC which was scheduled twice a week. Its primary mission was to evacuate military personnel from Djibouti or transiting US Navy ships, in need of medical attention not available at the base clinic. Its normal manifest, as space permitted, were military personnel rotating to their next duty assignment.

The plane was a Boing 737. Seating was modified to accommodate four stretchers by the forward galley. It was flown by a commercial airline under contract with the US Air Force. Unlike most Space-A flights, less than half the seats were occupied. I guess Djibouti was not an attractive destination.

We claimed three seats near the back, with Jabaal handcuffed to the window seat. The three of us slept most of the way to Rota. The box lunch served was a poor second to the one we had earlier on the MAC flight.

We were met in Rota by an RAF Gulfstream. No box lunches were provided, just cups of weak tea. Commander Milo met us at the RAF station in Lakenheath. We were whisked away to London, Jabaal to the local brig.

In our debrief with Commander Milo, Detective Chief Inspector Allenby, and Sir Charles, Sir Charles started with, "Your mission was a failure. Abandoned American weapons are now awash in the Horn of Africa."

"That's not…" I started before I was waved down.

"But I want to commend you for making the best out of a situation outside of your control," he continued.

"I didn't think we'd see Jabaal again; thought he'd drift into the Pakistani underworld," Chief Inspector Allenby. "Now to find Amal."

"Give it time," said Sir Charles. "Alexander tells me that Isabel's uncle has set his dogs loose to track him down," and under his breath,

I heard him mutter, "and there probably won't be much of him left for us."

24 The Search

After George and Harold left Beirut, Amal contacted some people he knew, putting a bounty on Amal Choucair. These weren't nice people, but he wanted the cur alive; he had his own idea for justice. So, he specified alive and an extra bonus for unharmed.

One of his old Syrian rivals, Ismail, after some research, thought he knew where Amal might be found, in Pakistan protected by the Pakistani Taliban. Why Pakistan? Afram Gurmani was born in Peshawar. He had uncles and cousins in a local Taliban splinter group. An uncle was a minor warlord.

Taking two of his trusted men, Ismail transited Iran in an old Isuzu Trooper. Amal had obtained travel documents from his contact in the Irian Revolutionary Guard, allowing them to cross Iran unmolested. After two days on poorly maintained roads, they arrived at Zahedan in eastern Iran where they spent the night at a flea-infested rest stop. They crossed into Pakistan at the Iran-Pakistan border crossing early the next morning. The crossing was facilitated by the IRG documents.

Following the Quetta-Taftan Highway, they passed just south of Afghanistan and late the next night, ended up in Bahadur Kalay, a small town on the outskirts of Peshawar. A room was available at the Shahi Palace Guest House, a discount hotel near the airport. This was their base of operations until they found Gurmani.

It wasn't hard finding Gurmani. A chance visit to the Peshawar Tea House on the north side of the airport found him holding court, bragging about being a member of the British Parliament.

Ismail left one of his men at the tea house telling him to follow Gurmani when he left. He and his other man would be parked down the street near a residential area.

It was about an hour later when Gurmani left. Walking down the street, Gurmani passed Ismail's parked SUV. Turning into the neighborhood he entered an apartment building. This was an area next to the Farabi Degree College with many students coming and going.

"This will be an easy place to grab him," said Ismail to his two companions. "There are several places we can watch from. I want you two to blend in and get a feeling for the area. I'll pick you up later."

Two days later Ismail made his move. Gurmani was walking to the tea house. One of Ismail's men was on foot in the back of Gurmani when the Isuzu pulled up. The second man jumped out, and Gurmani was forced into the SUV, a man on either side of him holding wicked-looking knives to his body.

The border crossing point back into Iran was a two-day drive. Ismail knew a retired smuggler living in Zehri, a small hamlet halfway to the border.

On their way north to Peshawar, Ismail had made arrangements, a bundle of cash with the promise of more, in exchange for a secure stopping point on their return trip.

All went well that night. In the morning, their host even provided tea and flatbread for their journey.

At the Pakistan-Iran checkpoint, the Iranians pulled Gurmani from the vehicle and 'gently' questioned him. Ismail, seeing the bounty slipping from his grasp, called Amal.

"This is Ismail. I have Gurmani, or rather, the Iranian border guards now have him. What should I do?"

"Sit tight. I'll take care of it."

Thirty minutes later there was a call from a senior member of the IRG. A visibly shaken border guard escorted Gurmani back to the vehicle and dumped him in. "The Irian Revolutionary Guard has placed your prisoner under their protection," he said.

The next thirty-six hours, with three uneventful border crossings, had Ismail and his passenger on the outskirts of Beirut.

"Amal, I have your package. I'm thinking it might be a good time to refresh our discussion about the bounty," Ismail said.

"What you want me to lower it?" laughed Amal. "If you are trying to hold me hostage for more money, I will harm your family. So. Let's keep this on a professional basis. I set the bounty. You found the package, and the bounty will be paid upon delivery."

After a moment's hesitation, Ismail asks where to deliver Gurmani.

***

Afram Gurmani sat tied to a chair in Amal's study.

"Afram, what am I going to do with you?" said Amal. "You have caused me and my business a great deal of problems. I think for the next day or two, I will hold you in the basement. I had a small cell constructed for these occasions. You might find the space cramped but sufficient for you to contemplate your fate. I was thinking about your demise; the one rumored for Edward II may be fitting. You know, the story about the hot poker up the bum."

"James," shouted Amal, "take our guest to his apartment."

The large man standing in the corner came forward, cutting his bindings, lifted Afram out of the chair, and dragged him from the room.

Amal Choucair sat quite contentedly behind his desk. He wanted to share his good spirits. He decided to call Alexander Basdakis.

"Alexander, you old dog, are you still tracking me?" After a bit of banter back and forth, Amal told Alexander he had Afram in his cellar. Please tell your nephew George that Afram is in good hands.

***

Two days later, locals reported unnatural screams in the early morning and of a lack SUV leaving the Choucair compound. The SUV was later seen at an upscale marina where a man-size package was loaded onto Mr. Choucair's yacht.

25 The Revelation

About the same time Amal was speaking with Alexander, Elana called Maggi. "At ltl George's birthday party, I gave big George his family's genealogy history. Since then, I did a little more digging to get the story of Isabel. George will want to know what I found; it could change the entire investigation he and Harold are working on."

"What did you discover?"

Elana told Maggi. "He will be stunned by this news," said Maggi, "he's still in his hotel room. Call him at this number."

When the phone rang, George was just putting on his jacket, getting ready to meet DI Lynn in the hotel lobby. "Maggi," he started to say when Elana blurted out, "You will never believe what I found. I was searching for Issabel's birth records and discovered she has an identical twin sister."

"What did you say," he said as he sat down.

Elana went on to tell him the details. "Isabell was born on June 10th, 1998, at the Royal Papworth Hospital in Cambridge," Elana said. "Her twin sister, Dina, was delivered five minutes later. I searched for Dina but found no additional information. She disappeared!"

"Are you sure about this?" George asked.

"It's in the official birth record database," said Elana. "It happened; the question is what became of Dina. There is no death record. The UK is a stickler in maintaining vital statistics."

"Elana, thank you for calling," said George. "This information may have just sent our investigation off on a new tangent."

George found Harold in the lobby looking at his watch. "About time you showed up," he said. "You look excited about something."

George sat in the lounge chair opposite Harold and repeated Elana's news.

Later at the MET DCI Allenby absorbed this new information, mulled it over for a moment before saying, "You two are going back to Cambridge to talk to the Baron. Tell him you want a credible answer or we will excavate his garden and yard looking for Dina's body."

* * *

Late that afternoon we arrived at the Baron's Grantchester estate, no notice of our pending visit. Rupert, surprised to see us, invited us in asking if we had new information on Isabell.

"Let's talk about Dina," I said.

Taken by surprised Rupert was hard pressed to put a coherent sentence together. Finally, "Who's Dina?"

"Issabel's twin sister," snapped Harold.

"I told you this would come out," said Nadine, who had just entered the room.

Perhaps you can enlighten us," I said.

Taking a deep breath, Nadine went on, "It was six months after the twin's birth, Dina's development started to suggest mental deficiencies. After a year she was declared to have a rare mental disorder. I don't recall what the doctors called it, but it was incurable.

83

My brother offered to take her to Lebanon where he could have her cared for. The National Health Service was no help. Dina ended up in a private clinic outside Beirut. I visited once when she was about two. It was painful; I never went back. Amal paid the bill, and over the years, she was mostly forgotten. As far as I know she is still there."

"Where is this clinic?" I asked.

"I don't recall, you have to ask Amal."

26 Twin

Driving back to London, Harold was mulling over Nadine's revelations. "I think a visit to Mr. Choucair is in order, preferably without prior notice," he said.

"Agreed. You get travel approval for us from Commander Milo; I need to call my Uncle in Athens."

As Harold navigated the government bureaucracy to get our travel approval, I called GSI. Getting the receptionist, I asked, "Is Mr. Basdakis in?".

"Yes, who should I say is calling."

"Mr. Basdakis."

"George," she said with a giggle, "I'll transfer you."

"Alexander here; what can I do for you, George?"

"First, did you know Elana discovered Isabell had a twin?"

"Yes, she told me shortly after she called you. I assume that's why you're back in England."

"Yes, my cousin Rupert confirmed it, or more precisely, his wife provided the details.

"Dina is Isabell's identical twin. She was born with a neurological defect. Uncle Amal offered to have the infant cared for. He took Dina to Lebanon and placed her in a private clinic. Nadine visited once when the girl was about two, but there was no further parental contact. To put it bluntly, Dina was little more than a mobile vegetable at that time.

"I suspect there is more to this story. Harold and I are returning to Beirut to continue our discussion with Amal. There is something fishy here. My question for you is, do you still have an agent in Beirut that I can use?"

After a short pause and rustling of paper, Alexander responds, "Yes, I have a young man there, Gregory, who is available. Give me your itinerary, and he will meet you at the airport."

***

Gregory met us at the airport, a young man, totally in the dark as to his mission.

I wanted a low-key meeting with Isabell's uncle, no call ahead. Harold and I left Gregory at a small coffee shop by the Greek Embassy. Commandeering the car, we made our way to Amal's compound.

Three of his men were manning the gatehouse and wanted to know our business.

"I'm George Basdakis, and this is Inspector Lynn. We met with Mr. Choucair to discuss his niece's death last month. We have a few follow-up questions. Is Mr. Choucair in?"

After the beefiest one made a call to the main house, we were allowed entrance. The butler was waiting for us at the main entrance.

"If you would follow me," he said, "Mr. Choucair is waiting for you in his study."

"George, what has it been, a month? Since your last visit? " Amal said, rising from his seat. Come, have a seat," he said, pointing to two plush chairs. "Coffee?"

Following the Mideast custom, we had coffee and talked a bit about trivial stuff. After five minutes, I set my coffee cup down and asked, "Tell us about Dina."

This clearly caught him by surprise. "Who is this Dina?" he asked.

"Isabell's twin. The one you have been caring for since her birth."

"It's a sad story," he said. "The poor girl was born with neurological deficiencies. Her parents did not have the means to care for her, and the British National Health Service was a joke. I offered to see to her care here in Lebanon. She is in a private clinic not far from here."

Can we visit her? I asked.

Why, she can't communicate; won't even know you're there.

It's just one last detail we need to document to close out our investigation of Isabell's murder.

If you insist, be here at noon tomorrow. My driver will take you to the clinic.

27 Dina

As promised, Amal's driver took us to the clinic, the Ayada Aladtrabat al-Asbia (Clinic for Neurological Disorders), where Dina was being cared for. It was a modern facility located in the Beirut foothills. The building itself had two floors and looked like it could accommodate thirty to fifty patients. The grounds were immaculate, with several patients in wheelchairs being pushed by attendants.

The driver told us to go in; he would wait in the car. As we walked in, the receptionist greeted us by name. Apparently, Amal notified the clinic of our visit.

"Mr. Basdakis, Mr. Choucair told us you'd be visiting Dina today. As I'm sure he explained, Dina is nonresponsive. We do our best to keep her clean, fed, and comfortable. She is in the private garden, getting some sun. If you go through that door, the path leads to the garden. Look for the attendant with the red scarf; she is waiting for you."

Harold and I did as directed and found ourselves in a walled garden set aside for special patients. The attendant with the scarf was on the far side with her patient sitting in a wheelchair in the dappled sun. She saw us, stood up, and waved.

"Mr. Basdakis, we've been expecting you. I told Dina you would be visiting. I believe Mr. Choucair said you were her cousin. It's so sad. She has no idea you are here, and I doubt she can understand us."

Harold and I sat on the bench opposite Dina and studied her. She looked remarkably like Isabell's pictures. I tried talking to her but got no reaction. After fifteen minutes, I thanked the attendant, and as Harold and I prepared to leave, one of the aids motioned for us to follow him as we returned to the reception area.

Looking over his shoulder, he said, "That's not Dina. Dina left here over a month ago. Mr. Choucair's men took her. This impostor arrived this morning. She was placed here for your visit." Turning down a side path, he was gone.

Riding back to the Choucair estate, Herold and I were mostly quiet. Once we were back in Gregory's car, Harold started to speak. I put my finger to my lips and whispered wait. Gregory later reported a listening device had been placed in the roof liner.

Suspecting Amal had bugged our hotel room, Harold and I found a small coffee shop and, after a brief discussion, agreed to table any further discussion until we were on the plane headed back to London.

Before leaving the next morning, I asked Gregory to find the young aide who talked with us. I provided his description and the name that was on the name tag, Mohammad.

***

Back in London, during our debrief with Commander Milo, Harold and I were convinced we did not see Dina. Herold said, "In addition to the story the aide told us on the way out, I observed that "Dina" was wearing two rings. This struck me as strange for someone in a vegetable state.

"I also noticed the jewelry, as well as her pierced ears," I said. "And did you notice how her eyes flickered when the aide mentioned I was her cousin?"

Milo's phone rang, it was Sir George. Milo listened, said, "I'll tell them," and hung up. He turned to us, "Alexander's man in Beirut reported this morning that the male aid you asked him to locate…was found dead this morning."

Commander Milo next expressed what I was thinking. "I don't think Isabell is dead. I think Dina was the body we found, and Isabell is in Beirut under Mr. Choucair's protection."

That's going to be bitch to prove, said Herold. There are several people providing positive identification of the body, including the parents, and a positive DNA match.

28 Aftermath

Six months later, the MET closed Isabell's case, labeling it unsolved.

Alexander's contacts reported Amal Choucair had stepped back from his many illicit operations, turning over day-to-day control to a young lady named Amira. Amira was an unknown to all his contacts, a body that came out of the woodwork, so to speak. She was also elusive; no one could get a photo of her.

On one of his routine visits to London, Alexander and Sir George speculated over a sniffer of twenty-year-old Scotch that Amira was the reincarnated Isabell. Scuttlebutt had it that she was a hard-nose negotiator.

On a more positive note, Harold and Elana had a thing going. After multiple trips to Greece, Harold convinced Elana she might give England a try; her genealogy business would be well received there.

END

www.ingramcontent.com/pod-product-compliance
Lightning Source LLC
Chambersburg PA
CBHW071338130626
46556CB00004B/1931